Florence Parry Heide & Roxanne Heide Pierce

TIMOTHY TWINGE

Illustrated by Barbara Lehman

Lothrop, Lee & Shepard Books   New York

Library of Congress Cataloging in Publication Data. Heide, Florence Parry. Timothy Twinge / by Florence Parry Heide and Roxanne Heide Pierce : illustrated by Barbara Lehman.   p.   cm.   Summary: Timothy Twinge, a fearful worrier, discovers his own bravery after meeting an unusual visitor. ISBN 0-688-10762-1.—ISBN 0-688-10763-X (lib. bdg.) [1. Worry—Fiction.   2. Fear—Fiction. 3. Courage—Fiction.   4. Stories in rhyme.]   I. Pierce, Roxanne Heide.   II. Lehman, Barbara, ill.   III. Title. PZ8.3.H412Ti 1993 [E]—dc20 91-39013 CIP AC

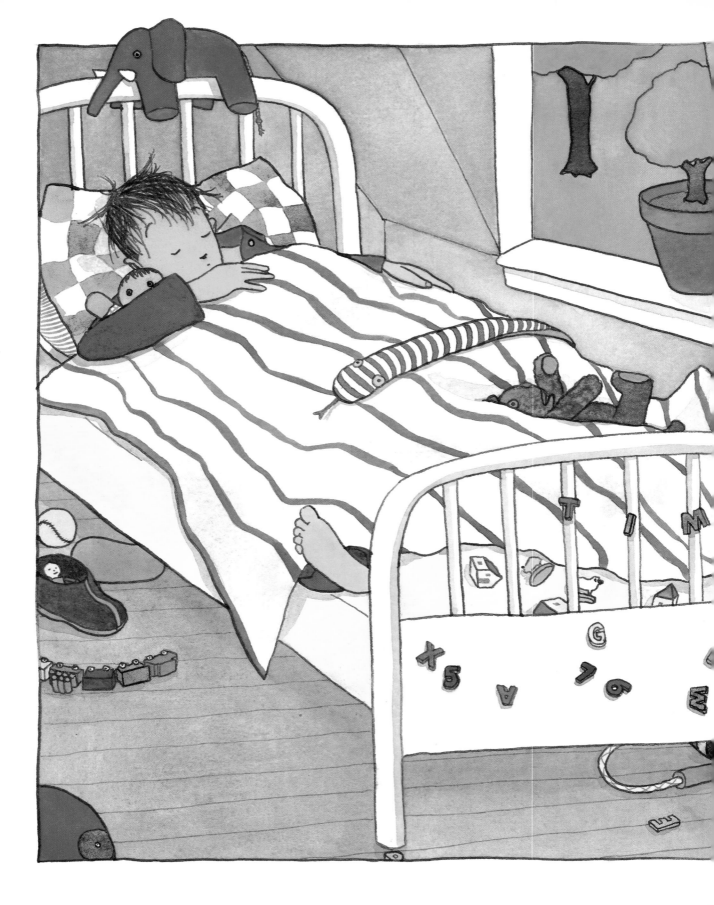

With much love to Heather
from Merm and Nainie

RHP and FPH

For the Boswells

BL

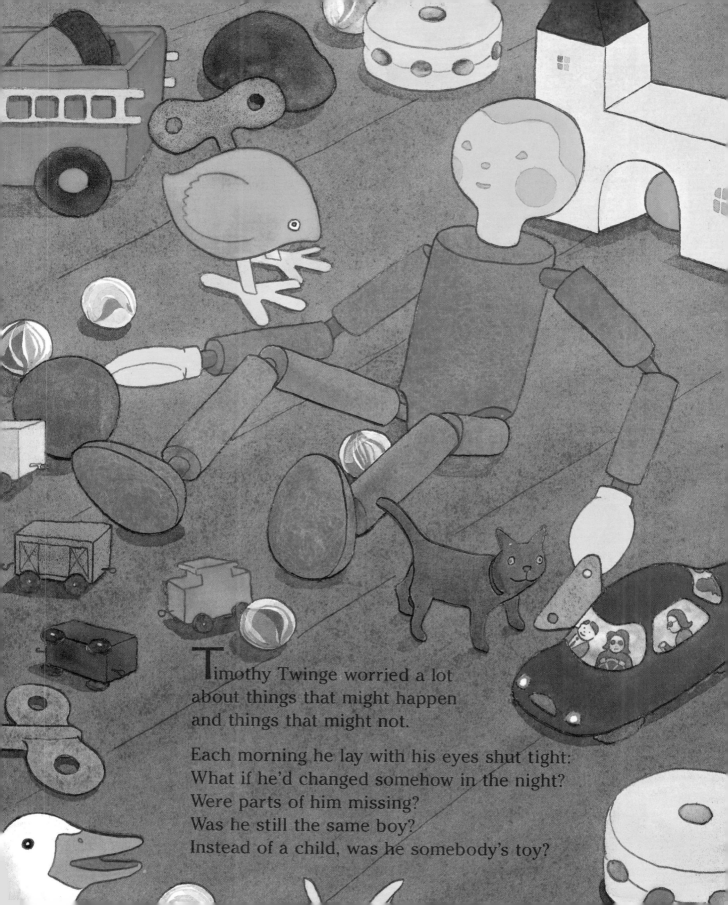

Timothy Twinge worried a lot
about things that might happen
and things that might not.

Each morning he lay with his eyes shut tight:
What if he'd changed somehow in the night?
Were parts of him missing?
Was he still the same boy?
Instead of a child, was he somebody's toy?

Or maybe he'd melted
drop by drop from his bed,
with nothing left of him now but his head.

He felt for his hands
and his legs
and his feet.
All there, after all.
Tim was complete!
But...

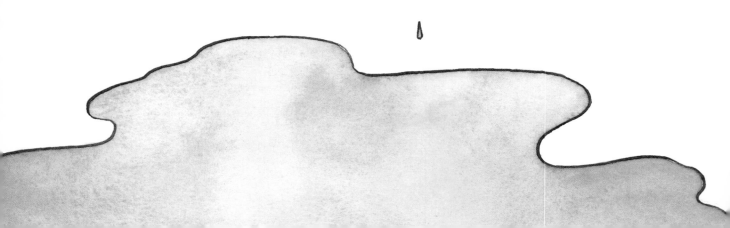

Perhaps it had rained
while he'd been asleep
until the water was ninety feet deep.
Maybe the house had drifted away
and would float like a boat for a week and a day.
There he'd be, tossed in the sea
for sharks to munch on hungrily.
He opened his eyes: same yard, same tree—
What a relief! He was safe—wasn't he?

Timothy slowly crawled out of bed
and tiptoed down the hall in dread.

Why did people seem to think
that faucets in the bathroom sink
would turn on *water* every time?
Someday something else might climb
through faucet pipes to grab and hold....
Would that thing be hot or cold?
He didn't like the thought of either,
so Timothy would turn on neither.
Hot or cold or lukewarm mixtures—
he stayed away from bathroom fixtures.

When Tim came down the stairs at last,
his feet were slow, his eyes downcast.
For breakfast there'd be raisin toast:
he really hated toast the most.
Those weren't raisins, they were bugs.
Roaches, maybe, or possibly slugs.

"Don't dawdle so!" his mother said.
"Hurry up, the day's ahead!
The sun is out—go play outside!"
But Tim did not feel qualified
to brave the world beyond the door.
Timothy Twinge didn't like to explore.

On sunny days he stayed inside—
Otherwise he might be fried
like an egg or dried like a prune,
all shriveled up in the afternoon.

Rainy days were equally scary:
Soggy grass made Tim feel wary.
Slippery things could hide in there
and grab his feet. He must beware.

While Timothy worried over *this*'s and *that*'s,
his mother suggested, "Let's get our hats."
Oh, no! That meant a trip to the store—
an errand that Tim would rather ignore.

It was not just the food that caused him to pause:
The shelves themselves were really flat jaws
that snatched at your hand if you reached back too far
to try to get hold of a different jar.

Home again finally, with bags to unload—
Tim worried, of course, that the cans would explode,
sending gobs of soup and olives and peas
all over the house . . . to attract killer bees.

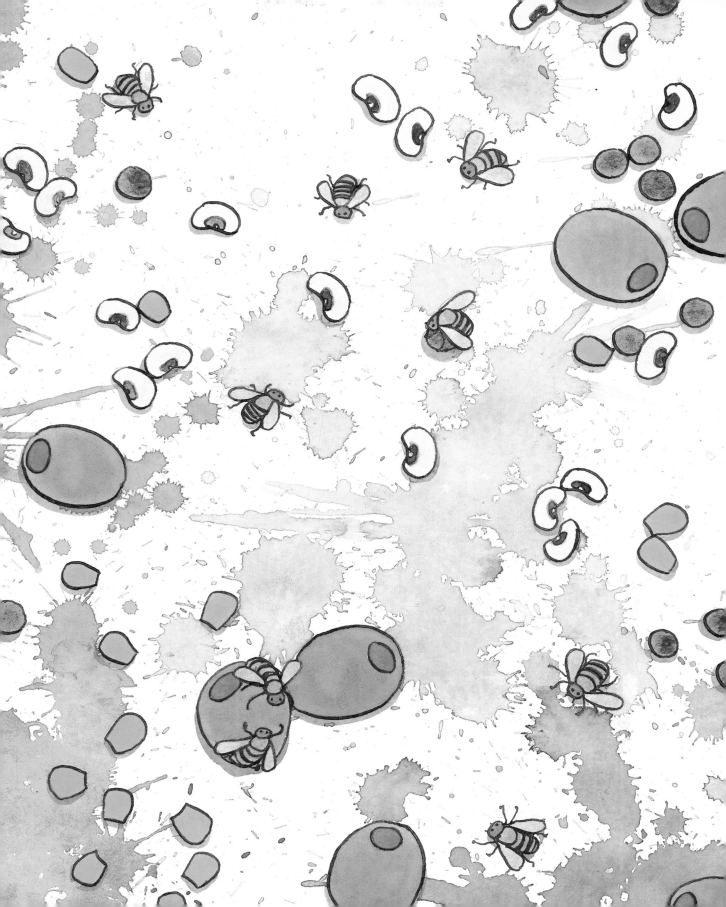

"Two hours till supper—find something to do.
Go read a book, dear, it's so good for you."

Maybe for others, Tim thought with chagrin.
With his luck, though, he'd likely fall in
and get trapped in the pictures and words on the page,
and there he would stay till he reached middle age.
He read with his eyes closed, just to be sure
(though it did make the story rather obscure).

"It's time to set the table, dear."
Tim wished that he could disappear.
Forks and knives and spoons just might
decide they had an appetite.
He pulled his hand out of the drawer.
How many fingers had he had before?

It was suppertime again for Tim;
his parents hovered over him.
Eating dinner...that sounds easy,
but macaroni made him queasy.
Noodles always made him squirm—
each one was a fat white worm
covered in something strange and sticky,
slimy, gooey, messy, icky.

After dinner, they watched TV.
To Tim it spelled catastrophe.
It could suck him in in two seconds flat!
Timothy Twinge really cringed at that.

He'd like a snack before going to bed—
peanut butter and jelly on bread.
But what was in the refrigerator?
Maybe he'd eat a little later,
after whatever was *in* got *out*
... and when it did, would it wander about?
Would it hide in the cupboard? under a chair?
Would it tiptoe at night or fly through the air?

The worst of all was still ahead:
It was time at last to go to bed.
Only at night did aliens fly!
This might be the night they'd try
to find his house, his window, his bed.
Oh, dear, thought Timothy,
I hope they've been fed.

Had they come tonight, those creatures from space?
He peered from his window, just in case.

And sure enough, there they were!
One of them said, "Good evening, sir!"

Why were they here? Was this some kind of game?
For monsters they certainly looked very tame.
Not fierce at all, just kind and nice.
"Good evening, sir." (They said it twice.)
"This is cause for celebration!
A human with imagination!

We've watched your thoughts go to and fro.
You're really braver than you know."
What? Tim gulped. Was this true?
Was he braver than he knew?
"No one else even guessed we existed.
Please be our friend," they all insisted.

"You could be our captain.
You could be our chief.
You could rule the galaxy!"
Said Timothy: "Good grief!"

Then off they flew into the night.
They waved goodbye—they *were* polite!
They looked like stars or fireflies.
Only Tim knew otherwise.

Timothy Twinge got ready for bed.
"I'm really important now," he said.
"That's an impressive thing to be—
the full-time Ruler of the Galaxy!
I'd better be brave," thought Timothy Twinge.
"I may even go on a raisin toast binge!"

He got to be brave—oh, very, very!
He got to be extraordinary.
He kept it a secret, and nobody knew
but Timothy Twinge—and now (of course) you.